MARVELLOUS MYTHS

EDITED BY LYNSEY EVANS

First published in Great Britain in 2024 by:

YoungWriters®
—————— Est. 1991 —

Young Writers
Remus House
Coltsfoot Drive
Peterborough
PE2 9BF
Telephone: 01733 890066
Website: www.youngwriters.co.uk

Printed and bound in the UK by BookPrintingUK
Website: www.bookprintinguk.com
YB0586N

FOREWORD

For our latest competition, The Glitch, we asked secondary school students to turn the ordinary into the extraordinary by imagining an anomaly, something suddenly changing in the world, and writing a story about the consequences. Whether it's a cataclysmic twist of fate that affects the whole of humanity, or a personal change that affects just one life, the authors in this anthology have taken this idea and run with it, writing stories to entertain and inspire. We gave them an added challenge of writing it as a mini saga which forces them to really consider word choice and plot. We find constrained writing to be a fantastic tool for getting straight to the heart of a story.

The result is a thrilling and absorbing collection of tales written in a variety of styles, and it's a testament to the creativity of these young authors, and shows us just a fraction of what they are capable of.

Here at Young Writers it's our aim to inspire the next generation and instil in them a love of creative writing, and what better way than to see their work in print? The imagination and skill within these pages show that we might just be achieving that aim! Congratulations to each of these fantastic authors, they should be very proud of themselves.

CONTENTS

Forest Oak School, Smiths Wood

Leo Hicks (11)	60
Serenity Whyte (12)	61
Scarlett Dyke (12)	62
Aaliyah Gourlay (11)	63
William Powers (11)	64
Jack Salmon (11)	65

King Edward VI Five Ways School, Bartley Green

Sharon Kenneth (11)	66
Freya Coombe	67
Reuben Singh Sangera Punia (12)	68
Joseph Mukoro (11)	69
Janani Kumara Gurubaran	70
Khaleeq Badmus (12)	71
Daniyel Oche (12)	72
Ellen Cheng	73
Shania Dadrah (12)	74
Shaurya Iyengar (11)	75
Hyabel Ukbit (12)	76

London East Academy, London

Samihuz Zaman (14)	77
Mahir Rahman (14)	78
Fhahad Ahmed (14)	79
Muhammad Alom (13)	80
Yahya Kasoma (14)	81
Riyad Dahbi (13)	82
Awwab Ibne-Razi (15)	83
Yahyaa Abdur Rahman (14)	84
Umar Mirza (13)	85
Ibraheem Hussain (13)	86
Ayaan Ahmed (13)	87

Queen Katharine Academy, Walton

Isabella Hollingsworth (13)	88
Dylan Murphy (11)	89
Kieran Hurdman (13)	90
Masey Long (12)	91

Edlin Elsa Edison (12)	92
Neelah Springthorpe (13)	93
Yenara Madanayaka (13)	94
Bella Marshall (13)	95
Kaci Marriott (12)	96
Destiny Price (12)	97
Juta Butvydaite (12)	98
Vanessa Sketrys (11)	99
Amelia-Mai Crick (13)	100
Mia Njeru (12)	101
Vanessa Sketrys (11)	102
Callum Baylis (13)	103
Khadija Ahmed (12)	104
Arfa Naveed (11)	105
Macey Mueller (11)	106
Jessie Stanley (11)	107
Theo Hollingsworth (11)	108
Lilly-Rose Beeny (14)	109
Mia Merrison (11)	110
Muskaan Shanzad (12)	111
Olivia Feerick (12)	112
Mario Tambura (12)	113
Antoni Mikucki (11)	114
Lilly Faull (12)	115
Kotryna Krutkeviciute (13)	116
Jayden Ross Santos De Sesto (13)	117
Zeinib Rahi (13)	118
Aniyah Rehman (11)	119
Daniel Sousa Loly (11)	120
Shania Hogan (12)	121
Jemima Adegunna (13)	122
Alayna Ahmed (11)	123
Annabelle Skingsley (12)	124
Safah Islam (13)	125
Harry Roddis (12)	126
Maizie Howley-Burke (13)	127
Emily French (11)	128
Dovidas Grigor Jevas (12)	129
Logan Harradine (12)	130
Harry Boyce (11)	131
Michael Cavanagh (13)	132
Raheel Kazim (14)	133
Laibah Arif (11)	134

Willow Smith (11)	135	Sami Rahman (14)	176
Maya Zasada (12)	136	Zaira Harris (13)	177
Eryk Hoscilowicz (11)	137	Karim Isli (13)	178
Minahil Tahir (12)	138		
Evie Feerick (13)	139		
Dejvi Alijaj (13)	140		
Liya Tawfeq (11)	141		
Ummayyah Ali (12)	142		
Olivia-Mae Brudenell (12)	143		
Alastair Green (12)	144		
Tuaha Saqib (12)	145		
Sofie Hollis (13)	146		
Gracie-May McGill (12)	147		
Bella Nicholls (13)	148		
Spencer Currie (13)	149		
Ricardo Christie-Mpitu (13)	150		
Tommy-Lee Gates (12)	151		
Liam Wright (13)	152		
Evie McKimmie (12)	153		
Kayla Kelly (12)	154		
Renata Ciumac (14)	155		
Aden Makauskas (13)	156		
Dainton Tee (14)	157		
Evie Bass (12)	158		
Regina Phiri (13)	159		
Taylor Baines (13)	160		
Denisa Dorobantu (13)	161		
Cadi Balde (13)	162		
Aayan Shahid (14)	163		
Kaylub Thurston (13)	164		
Cerys Jenner (13)	165		
Wiktor Wilk (13)	166		

Regent High School, Camden

Ejaz Khan (14)	167
Abdul Yahya (13)	168
Angelica Kazankova (14)	169
Shezmin Begum (13)	170
Sara Ahmed (13)	171
Maya Ullah (14)	172
Kassim Kassim (14)	173
Immanuel Chella (13)	174
Sannah Yaqub (14)	175

THE STORIES

THE GLITCH

In the quiet futuristic city, a glitch rippled through the augmented reality network. Buildings distorted, skies fractured. Sam, an ordinary commuter, found reality bending around him. The glitch granted unexpected powers and temporal jumps. Bewildered, he leapt through time, witnessing history's untold moments. Each jump reshaped his understanding. As he grappled with the glitch, Sam discovered a hidden world beyond the visible where glitches were gateways to enlightenment. In embracing the unpredictable, he transcended the confines of normality. The glitch, once a disturbance, became a cosmic brush painting new dimensions across the canvas of Sam's existence. After that, he was never seen.

Charlie Leitch
Berwick Academy, Spittal

THE UNEXPLAINED ATTACK OF 2050

I was standing outside having a drink when out of nowhere a massive shock happened. The ground shook and everybody started panicking. A massive, round, pointy object was flying at us.

Then it happened... a blast. Everything was destroyed.

The sun hadn't risen for five years. The survivors had all woken and we all approached the object.

It was a nuke with an unknown flag on it!

We were suddenly being invaded. Foreign soldiers were everywhere! We were being overrun... until a bright blue light lit the ruined town up.

The invaders disappeared. The whole town was back to normal. Back in time...

Enrico Bevevino (14)
Berwick Academy, Spittal

DRAWINGS

Her drawings predicted the future. Every sketch was enchanted and told a story that was going to happen. The girl drew for hours, getting ideas into her head until it was stuffed.

One day, she drew something amazing, something nobody had ever thought of before.

She published it and it went worldwide and gained everyone's attention.

You're probably wondering what the painting was.

It was a beautiful sunset on a beach in Spain, except she put a location on the top right-hand corner but the location in Spain never existed, nor did the beach.

Everyone was weirded out by this conspiracy.

Olivia Currie (13)
Berwick Academy, Spittal

THE STRANGER

The car sprinted and wheezed before conking out on the side of the A697. It was dark, and there was a storm approaching. A silhouetted figure walked over the brow of the hill. It was tall, too tall. Its eyes, oh, its eyes were glowing red like the sunset on a winter's evening. He got out of the car, looking furious.

He opened the car door and exclaimed, "Dammit!" as he kicked the tyres.

It was only then that he saw the fast-approaching figure.

"What?" he stammered. "But, how? You're supposed to be dead!"

Suddenly, everything stopped. Nothing remained.

Alistair Nuttall (13)
Berwick Academy, Spittal

THE MIRROR MATRIX

It was Christmas morning, and Tabitha was so excited as she got her new mirror. Once it was put into her room, Tabitha had a weird feeling each time she walked by. She had to get ready for Christmas dinner, so she stood in front of the mirror. Then, her reflection put their forefinger to their mouth and that's when Tabitha heard a long haunting, "Shhhhh." The mirror started to crack, leaving her reflection distorted and Tabitha was left unable to speak. Tabitha scurried downstairs and pointed at her mouth, but everyone stared at her like she had gone insane.

Eva Rybowska (13)
Berwick Academy, Spittal

BACK AGAIN

We buried it, but it was back. The old legend warned us of its persistence, but we thought we had defeated it. Years ago, we had concealed the cursed artefact deep within the earth, hoping it would never resurface. Yet, here it was, mocking our feeble attempts to bury the past. Its malevolent presence grew stronger: spreading darkness wherever it went. We knew we had to confront it once more. Armed with determination, we gathered courage and prepared for the battle ahead, determined to banish the ancient evil once and for all and finally reclaim peace for the town.

Imogen Borthwick
Berwick Academy, Spittal

THE DEMONIC DRAWINGS

The drawings predicted the future.

I was babysitting a girl and I realised she liked drawing as she had drawings all over her room. I gave her a set of coloured pencils and her face lit up with happiness; it made me feel warm inside. She drew a man standing behind another. I asked, "Who is that?" but she pointed at me. I said, "Oh, and who's the other?"

"Look behind you," she replied in a demonic tone.

My face went cold and chills ran down my spine as I felt breath on my neck. I turned around... *Slice.*

Tyler Portues (14)

Berwick Academy, Spittal

DROWNING LIGHTS

The sun hadn't risen for five years, but since the first day, there were strange lights in the ocean going back and forth. They seemed to sort of lure people. Their eyes rolled back in their heads and they just collapsed. Soon after there was another light in the ocean, although on social media everything seemed normal. Everyone was fine. Sun up and no lights in the ocean. Yet we were stuck here barely able to find water and eventually, we got used to it. Until the lights started walking.

Hold on, this is a... Argh! Look into the light now!

Joe Gill (14)

Berwick Academy, Spittal

IT'S BEHIND YOU

It was midnight, I was walking home from my nightshift with only the dull glow of the streetlights. That's when I heard it. A scream filled with shrill terror, it was coming from the park, it had been closed for years and was now overgrown. Not being able to see from this angle, I went to investigate and after a few minutes of searching, I found a woman mumbling quietly. I dragged her out into the light. When she finally looked up, her eyes full of terror, she whispered to me slowly, "It's behind you." The streetlights snapped off...

Jessica Deans (13)
Berwick Academy, Spittal

CASSIE

Cassie is travelling to Mars. She steps out of her rocket, and all of a sudden, she's transformed. Cassie is starting to panic. *What's going on?* She's there on her own. Cassie steps back into the rocket and suddenly becomes human again. She steps back out and transforms into a big, furry, blue monster. She leaps back into the rocket in a panic. Cassie is scared; she doesn't know what is going on. She travels back to Earth after all this time, for nothing. When Cassie gets back to Earth, she never speaks of this to anyone.

Abbie Crooks (13)
Berwick Academy, Spittal

GONE FOREVER

It was a dark night and Sarah was listening to music in her room. There was an eerie feeling in her room. She could feel eyes on her, but that didn't stop her from dancing and having a good time. After a while, she thought she heard her mother shouting her, so she went downstairs. Her mum wasn't down there, but she could hear something moving about. She searched the whole house until suddenly, something grabbed her. Sarah started fighting but it would not let her go. All that was heard was a blood-curdling scream. She was gone forever.

Caelin Farish (13)
Berwick Academy, Spittal

THE FANTASY MIRROR

If I'm being honest, I have no idea how I'm here. Let's start from the beginning.
I was at my friend Milly's house on Friday the 13th at 11:53pm. We started talking about a new app. I downloaded it, ignoring the signs and waited... I laughed it off and looked back at Milly, to find she wasn't there. Quickly, I turned around frozen with fear to find my reflection moving. And now I'm here in a dark room that looks as though light has *never* touched it. Now I look through a window that used to be a mirror.

Ava Walsh (13)
Berwick Academy, Spittal

THE ACCIDENT

We buried it, but it was back! How is that possible? Five years have passed since that awful night. I remember it was a stormy night. Lightning hit my car, and I skidded off the road, hitting and killing a man. He was the strangest-looking person; almost alien-like. I panicked and put the body in my car. The next day I buried the body in my garden and planted a tree. Now five years, to the exact date, he is staring at me, through my kitchen window. What does he want? Revenge?
I then wake up confused on the cold, hard floor.

Chloe Armstrong (14)
Berwick Academy, Spittal

THE OLD MAN

Once upon a time, there was a very, very old man who was an expert in all martial arts. He was so good that no one could beat him. Everyone but one person. A very peculiar boy. He was so fast that no one could catch him and so powerful no one could take his punches.
One day, the boy challenged the man and he accepted. Their battle was fast and furious, but eventually, the old man beat the boy with no scratch on him. The boy cried, "Who are you?"
The man chuckled and said, "I'm a god, boy..."

Tom Reid (13)
Berwick Academy, Spittal

BASED ON A TRUE STORY OF STAN, THE ESCAPING DOG

Stan was gone! Where was he? I searched high and low, but he was gone. The window was broken open and Stan was gone. We looked at his tracker, and he wasn't far away. I could see him; he was running. We caught a glimpse of his tail wagging excitedly. We dashed through the cornfield, but he was too fast. I screamed loudly, "Stan!" He just kept going. We found a pile of feathers, we knew he was not far away. We saw big paws in the air. It was Stanley. I jumped on him, we got him. What a relief.

Jack Bexon (14)
Berwick Academy, Spittal

UNTITLED

Sofia was a tall, popular, nasty girl.
One day, when she was at her local public park she and her friends found a bronze necklace. Sofia put it on. She wore it all day and went to take it off for bed. But as she was getting into bed it was on her neck again. Sofia woke up the next morning and took the necklace off before school. Once she arrived it was on again. She tried to get rid of the necklace as much as she could. It just reappeared on her neck again every time she took it off.

Ellie Hargreaves (13)
Berwick Academy, Spittal

EVERYONE IS GONE...

"You're early," said Death, "what happened?"
I was startled by the question, but then I noticed something peculiar. People around me were vanishing into thin air, one by one. The more people disappearing meant more people queueing up behind me.
"What's happening?"
Panic filled the air as confusion filled the crowd.
"I don't know," I replied, my voice quivering.
"Everyone is disappearing!"
Death was puzzled as chaos was unfolding. It was as if the future was unfolding before our eyes. We all just stood there, questioning what just happened, wondering if there was any way to reverse it. But there's not.

Koebii Robertson (13)
Brownedge St Mary's Catholic High School, Bamber Bridge

IT'S JUST ME

I wake up to see Mum gawping at me, a stunned expression on her face. I fret, suspecting something wrong. "M-Mum, what's wrong?" I fearfully question.
"Oh, honey, you're stunning, taking my breath away!"
I ran to my mirror and stared at my transformed reflection. A case of ugly-to-pretty overnight. I thought about school; everyone would be envious. My teacher would actually pay attention to me. My bully wouldn't be mean to me anymore. My life was beginning to brighten with a shining light. A silent, whispery voice said, "Your looks don't matter, it's you that matters... watch out."

Jiya Deol (12)
Brownedge St Mary's Catholic High School, Bamber Bridge

UNTITLED

"You're early," said Death. "What happened?"
My brain couldn't process anything.
"Child, what happened?"
His voice grew sterner, deeper, more menacing.
"I, all I remember is fire."
Death stared at me with terror on his face.
"No, no, not yet. This can't happen." He began rummaging through drawers of a desk that had suddenly appeared as if out of thin air.
"Not enough time. Too much to do." He slammed the drawer shut, the sound lost in the void around us. He pulled out a file. On it a living picture of a world burned to a crisp.

Lily Chalmers (13)
Brownedge St Mary's Catholic High School, Bamber Bridge

YOU'RE NEXT

"Hi, is anyone still here?" I screamed. No reply! A letter at my door said, 'You are late. Everyone is already dead but you. We need you and then we're finished, so hurry up - Death'.

"Stop messing with me, Mum!" I bellowed whilst running away. I swung open my friend's door. "Anyone home?" No reply. "Stop messing with me, please just reply." No reply! I went to the police station... no one was there! I saw someone. I started running towards them but it wasn't someone, it was a pole.

'If you're reading this, you're next. Don't test me - Death'.

Aoife Wildman (11)
Brownedge St Mary's Catholic High School, Bamber Bridge

THE GLITCH

Stanley was a gamer boy. He'd never stop gaming. His favourite thing to do was play war games.

One night, while he was on his computer, he encountered a message. The message said, 'Update'. Next to it said in bold, 'Warning!'

Ignoring the warning he updated it.

The next morning he went downstairs to eat breakfast. Nothing seemed normal.

"Dad!" he shouted.

Nobody was there.

Boom! Out of nowhere, a fiery explosion rose into the air. The smoke was as dark as one thousand midnights. That's when he realised he wasn't living in reality. He was in a simulation.

Arthur Pinder (11)
Brownedge St Mary's Catholic High School, Bamber Bridge

THE MONSTER'S ENCORE

We buried it, but it was back. The dreadful, grim and horrid creature. We thought we had gotten rid of it, for good. But it was back and this time it looked famished, thirsting for blood.

Twenty years ago...

"Mum! The ice cream truck is here!" I shouted from across the room.

"So what if it's here?" Mum said sarcastically.

"Please, Mum. Pretty please?" I begged.

"Okay! Stop begging!"

"Yay!" I screamed, like I'd won the lottery. But little did I know, that the moment I stepped outside my house, I was never coming back.

Hannah Vinod (13)

Brownedge St Mary's Catholic High School, Bamber Bridge

MALFUNCTION MIRROR

There was an eerie object in the darkness of the wood, a mirror. The mirror was florescent and blue like a wormhole or a portal. When I looked closer, I could see a reflection, but it wasn't me. It had holes in its slender arms and rawboned legs, and it smiled with blood drooling. It made me shudder in fear. Outside, thunder boomed, lightning crackled. *Do I walk through?* Then, something impossible happened. These bony, spindly hands pulled me in. Precipitously, I fell down, down, into this blood-curdling, sludgy hole with malicious chuckles that filled the tense and creepy atmosphere.

Ava Morgan (12)
Brownedge St Mary's Catholic High School, Bamber Bridge

THE GLITCH

The girl woke up and thought she was hallucinating. She called her mum to come upstairs. When her mum arrived upstairs, a horrid scream came out. "What... what has happened? Our house, our city. We need to evacuate, now!" she yelled with fear. The girl saw suspicious men lurking around New York City with white masks on as if they were hackers... The girl and her mum were shocked, but then, Mum changed. She stopped and asked, "Who are you?" The girl's face went pale. She grabbed her mum's shoulders and said, "I am your daughter." Immediately, her mum ran away...

Callie-Jo Gray (11)
Brownedge St Mary's Catholic High School, Bamber Bridge

THE GLITCH

The sun hadn't risen in five years... The land had turned into an abandoned, frosty place where only monsters lived... cruel, blood-sucking monsters. It was a normal day with the monsters and moon until something catastrophic happened. The sun... the sun was rising! The beasts roared and took shelter, but the sun wasn't bright and yellow. It was like a glitch. All the grim colours were mixing together, but the sun wasn't normal... They had to figure out what was happening. It looked like the sky took envy on them... They came to an agreement, knowing what had happened...

Summer-Rose Calvert (11)
Brownedge St Mary's Catholic High School, Bamber Bridge

THE MALFUNCTION

One year ago, ignoring all of the red lights, I continue on my way.
The building shakes. I duck but nothing happens. Daring to look up, my mouth opens and I see glass hovering in mid-air.
My friend says, "It looks like a glitch."
I answer, "But how, we are not in a game?"
Although I know she is right about that, I still can't believe what I am hearing or seeing. It sounds crazy.
"Quick! Run!" she shouts.
As soon as I see it, I bolt. The shards of glass are falling, almost hitting us.
What is happening?

Mia Haynes-Williams (11)
Brownedge St Mary's Catholic High School, Bamber Bridge

THE GLITCH

I didn't move, but my skeleton did.

I was creating a skeleton for Halloween on my computer, but suddenly, it appeared. A message on my computer, a message saying 'follow me'.

Do I, or do I not?

I followed it. Instantaneously, the skeleton disappeared, and I followed its shadow. I opened the door to go outside and I couldn't see my eyes. There were dead bodies all over the floor and skeletons walking everywhere. I walked down the path and I saw a big pile of dead bodies and some became skeletons. They disappeared. It appeared. Suddenly, I was travelling.

Amelia Blaney (11)

Brownedge St Mary's Catholic High School, Bamber Bridge

UNTITLED

"The world is going to end... What do we do... They will get us..."

"It's only us left."

Beep, beep.

His alarm went off. "We need to go home, now, before the sun goes down!" He put the steel shutters on the windows and doors so they couldn't get him... Morning came. They rushed outside and tried to find a way to turn the zombies human. Before they knew it, it was dark. They rushed home but they got him. He was bleeding but escaped. They followed him back home and tried to get into the lab with a bomb.

Blast!

Gracie OHagan (11)

Brownedge St Mary's Catholic High School, Bamber Bridge

SCHIZOPHRENIA

I didn't move, but my reflection did. Wait, am I hallucinating? She was confused and fear was pumping through her anatomy. *Impossible, how could this be? Is there a glitch in my reality or dimension? Did I open a portal?* She was unaware and naive. She started thinking her life was a simulation. She wouldn't realise the truth, not without help. Her dilemma was futile. She was becoming apathetic. In her eyes, all she thought was it was just a dream or an error in her world. She won't believe the truth. She has schizophrenia. She's in denial.

Kiera Daubney (12)
Brownedge St Mary's Catholic High School, Bamber Bridge

ECLIPSE OF HOPE

The sun hadn't risen in five years, casting our world into an eternal twilight. Devastation consumed the city, and hope seemed like a distant memory. But among the darkness, a flicker of light lit within us. We united together, forging a community that refused to surrender. Through our unity, we fought to unravel the mystery behind the sun's disappearance. With each passing day, we uncovered fragments of forgotten knowledge, inching closer to a solution. And just when all seemed lost, a glimmer of light pierced the sky, signalling the dawn of a new chapter...

Maizie-Mae Nickson (13)
Brownedge St Mary's Catholic High School, Bamber Bridge

THE NIGHT

The stadium atmosphere was crazy, with bright lights and loud chants. Besides all of that, the best thing for him was the crowd chanting his name.

"Tyrene Campbell, Tyrene Campbell."

It was the playoff final 2-2. He scored two for his team and city. All of a sudden, the other team started walking into the dressing room. It was like a malfunction. A blue ring appeared on the pitch. It was like a portal. All of a sudden, the lights were flickering. The crowd disappeared and appeared again. It was like a glitch. It was too silent. It was an...

Harry Cranshaw (11)
Brownedge St Mary's Catholic High School, Bamber Bridge

THE REFLECTION

I got home from school and I went into my room; something didn't seem right. I shook. I looked in the mirror and my reflection moved when I didn't. I cried for help.

I went into the front room. My family was dead. 3am, 13th October, locked in my bathroom, crying. I tried to call 999 but the internet was down. I was trapped!

I heard a knock. He knew I was there. I started to lose my sanity and opened the door to my fate.

"Welcome to the underworld," said a strange voice. I was surrounded by fire. "Unlucky," it said.

Hollie Curwen (11)
Brownedge St Mary's Catholic High School, Bamber Bridge

THE RIFT

"You're early," said Death, "what happened?" He had a puzzled face when he said this.

I said, "Time collapsed on itself, the past, the present and future caved in on itself. It began eight years ago when the rift appeared. The same rift that corrupted my mother. We sealed the entity in a copper box. At the time, copper was its weakness, but somehow, it broke out. This time, it was vengeful. Very vengeful. It proceeded to warp more and more of time, leaving chaos in its path, using human life as a catalyst. Then..."

Jack Smith (13)
Brownedge St Mary's Catholic High School, Bamber Bridge

FROZEN MOMENTS

Every clock had stopped. So had time, but for some strange reason, I hadn't.

As I tried to work out what had happened, I wandered through the frozen streets.

It wasn't like a scene out of a horror movie - it was worse!

I went back to my house to see if my parents were frozen, but they were nowhere to be found, so I went to the basement.

I saw something much worse than frozen parents. I saw my dad's frozen hand pressed down on a button that read, 'Stop time forever'.

I knew that something was very wrong...

Xan Venables (13)

Brownedge St Mary's Catholic High School, Bamber Bridge

THE RED MIRROR

I didn't move, but my reflection did. I almost missed it; a flicker out of the corner of my eye. A fault. A glitch. A grin. I froze, my head half turned away from the mirror, my trembling hands still clutching the faucet, water still running. Again. There was something glinting in my pocket. Its pocket. We were unmoving, but it was smiling and I was staring. Again. Overwhelming, frigid fear swept through me like cold water, sharp and smiling, just like it. Panic consumed me, and with a jolt of adrenaline, I turned to run. But it was there.

Ethan Gardner (12)
Brownedge St Mary's Catholic High School, Bamber Bridge

FROZEN

I didn't move, but my reflection did. I woke up and looked in the mirror, but my reflection had not moved. I looked out of the window and everyone was frozen. I was confused. What had happened? Everything stopped, except for me. All the cars had stopped. All vehicles had stopped. All clocks had stopped. Everything but for me. It was a glitch. What had happened? It was impossible. It was like we were living in a simulation. It was so strange. Nothing moved. It was like I was alone and could not do anything. But then I saw something move.

Seth Boardman (12)
Brownedge St Mary's Catholic High School, Bamber Bridge

UNTITLED

Ignoring the warnings, I downloaded the app, thinking that it was probably a mistake.

One morning, I woke up for school, and an app popped up on my phone. I never thought that would be one of the worst decisions of my life. Behind my screen, there was somebody who knew everything. I had never been this scared. My hands were shivering. They knew where I lived, they knew my school, and they knew my email. They were out for me!

One night, there was somebody following me down the street with a knife. I sped up, and so did he...

Stacey Mclaughlin (12)
Brownedge St Mary's Catholic High School, Bamber Bridge

UNTITLED

Suddenly, I was travelling through time.

I had just gotten my first phone. I was excited to start using it. I was only eight. What did I know about technology? I didn't know anything, but I didn't care. I went ahead and started downloading stuff that I didn't know. I saw a friend-making app and I thought, *why not download it? I barely have any friends.* I signed up and put in my personal details. As I clicked save I immediately got sucked into it. I was scared.

Suddenly, I was travelling through time...

Deborah Kalaiyo (11)
Brownedge St Mary's Catholic High School, Bamber Bridge

AM I NEXT?

Imagine getting home from school and your house is empty, hours go by and still, nobody turns up. The phone rings... sounds like heavy breathing, "Hello," I say, but get no answer. I try to go to bed, I calm myself, "It's just a dream," I say. The dawn approaches but still, the house is vacant. My family isn't here, I have no idea what to do. Should I call someone for help or sit wondering? All day the silence is haunting and takes the life out of me but then, next, I hear a tug at the door...

Mollie Mae Hindle (11)
Brownedge St Mary's Catholic High School, Bamber Bridge

THE END OF TIME

This was it. The Earth was dead, but I could save it. Leaping over the molten lava, this was it. The beast's lair. It was terrifying. A dark cloud loomed overhead. Cautiously, I entered and found the beast. An intense battle, which lasted ages, commenced. The beast was strong, but I was stronger. After what seemed like ages, I won, but I had to save the world. So I looked for something, anything. I looked long and hard, and after what felt like an eternity, I found it. A key... A key to save time and the world.

Michael Shone (11)

Brownedge St Mary's Catholic High School, Bamber Bridge

THE COMPUTER

I was walking home, and I saw an old computer. I got home and plugged in the computer. When I went to the kitchen, I couldn't see my family anywhere. I shouted for them, and there was no answer. Then, I saw a flicker. I was confused. It seemed like my family had disappeared.

I went back to where the computer was, but it felt like it was another dimension. I was so confused. Everything looked different. I thought I was in a simulation or maybe a dream. I was confused. My fear kicked in, and then, I realised...

Luke Yates (12)

Brownedge St Mary's Catholic High School, Bamber Bridge

THE STRANGE WORLD

The world generated; everyone loaded and they were all cubes and rectangles. It was all blocky. It was scary. I could see ten hearts and ten chicken legs in the corner of my eye and never left. Everyone looked confused. Then I sprinted but I just realised that all chicken legs drained. Then I got hungry. Then it turned dark and lots of creatures appeared out of nowhere. Then one that looked like a a skeleton shot at one of my friends. Then he died. Then my hearts were now one. Then I got shot but I died to a zombie.

Dalton Green (11)
Brownedge St Mary's Catholic High School, Bamber Bridge

THE DAY THE WORLD WENT MAD

It was a normal Wednesday morning in the cold days of November. I went to school as per usual but something terribly wrong was going to happen. I was sitting in English trying to listen to the teacher. I did not get much of it so my eyes wandered out the window when I saw a group of students outside doing their PE lesson when something terrible happened... One of the girls disappeared but she did not just disappear, she teleported to our classroom. Now you don't know where you will teleport or where you will go.

Pippa Myerscough (11)
Brownedge St Mary's Catholic High School, Bamber Bridge

THE APP

Ignoring the warnings, I downloaded the app. It was a stupid, silly app that told you when you'd die, as if! It downloaded. I opened the app to a warning.
It read, 'You will die in two hours in a car crash'.
At first, I had a wave of worry, but that soon passed. I laughed it off and watched a movie. An hour later I got a phone call saying to avoid cars until the morning. I ignored it and just watched the movie.
Then my mum shouted, "Honey, get in the car!"
It was too late.

Daisy Johnstone (12)
Brownedge St Mary's Catholic High School, Bamber Bridge

THE LAST VISIT

A teenage boy went into a forest alone. He thought it would be a good idea to go further into the forest. Suddenly, the world around him went black. He thought the sun hadn't shown. He was lost and worried because he went further into the forest. The trees looked familiar. He had no phone. He thought he knew the way, but he didn't.

He saw an old beat-up mirror propped up by a tree. He looked into it and didn't move, but his reflection did. That was the last time anyone was seen in that forest.

Naomi Taylor (12)
Brownedge St Mary's Catholic High School, Bamber Bridge

ANTI-HACKERS

I moved, but my reflection didn't. Suddenly, everyone and everything was frozen in place except me. At first, everything was great. I could do, eat and drink anything, but then it happened... I was in the glitch with someone and got given powers and teleported to their world with everyone. Then I yelled at one of the hackers and they got deleted. I tried again. It didn't work. I went to this lab with five other people and we busted out and we are trying to stop them. We are called the Anti-Hackers.

Prince Nyamutora (11)
Brownedge St Mary's Catholic High School, Bamber Bridge

THE VIRUS

We buried it, but it was back.

The small, scared girl was running home from school. The 100-year-old virus was back and worse than ever. People were dying all over the city. People were fighting to survive. It started a war...

The dark, dismal sky covered the Earth. She was running like she never had before. She stopped in her tracks as she realised bombs had started to go off. Her home, her sweet, cosy home, was destroyed. Her whole family was gone. That was the moment she gave up...

Elsie Barron (12)
Brownedge St Mary's Catholic High School, Bamber Bridge

WHERE HAS THE SUN GONE?

The sun hadn't risen in years. My life had now adapted to the darkness which was now in every part of everyone's life. I thought this was a problem of climate change, but now it seemed like a real-life glitch. Not only had I lost hope, but everyone around too. However, one day, I got a feeling. A feeling of hope, and my body took over and I ran off with a torch in my hand. But I crashed with something almost like a door handle and as I began to twist and pull, a gust of wind and light hit...

Gabriel Nawrocki (12)
Brownedge St Mary's Catholic High School, Bamber Bridge

THE GLITCH

The glitch...
Suddenly, I travelled through time through some sort of portal. I was so confused. I was in the future. I pressed one button on my screen and typed up an error in red writing. I made it to this room with lots of computers and there seemed to be some hackers in these creepy masks.
They said, "If you finish this test, you can go."
So, I finished the test, and they sent me back through this crazy hologram portal. It was like magic. I still think I was dreaming...

Armani Dipalma (11)
Brownedge St Mary's Catholic High School, Bamber Bridge

THE DOOR

In the crack of my door, I see a dark, three-legged creature, staring at me with bright white teeth. Shivers ran through my body as it walked closer and closer to me. I rubbed my eyes and it was gone, but the breeze of death roamed around my room. But I could still hear chuckles around my room. The smell of murder was right under my nose. I felt slender fingers gliding up my arm. I jumped up in horror, turned to my left and there was nothing there. Shivers went around my body. Then, I woke up.

Ellie-May Vas (12)
Brownedge St Mary's Catholic High School, Bamber Bridge

THE GLITCH

I finished my food, ran upstairs to my room, and sat down on my bed. As I was wiping the breadcrumbs off my face, suddenly, my phone made a noise. I looked, and a random number had texted me. I cautiously opened the message, but, at the time, little did I know that would be the worst mistake of my life. There was a link; I opened it and ran downstairs to tell my mum. I looked at her in shock as she was frozen in mid-air. That link had frozen time, and I was the subject of this experiment.

Layton Proctor (12)
Brownedge St Mary's Catholic High School, Bamber Bridge

UNTITLED

Ignoring the warnings, I downloaded the app. Then, seconds later, I heard banging on my door. I went to go look but it was too late. I fainted. A couple of hours later, I woke up in a room with a type of uniform on. It was a room with a chair... Then, a worker person came in and gave me an odd-looking slice of pizza. I can remember that he injected it with something and I felt sick after. I can also remember a door that people went into and never came out of. It's my turn next. Help!

Alfie Hall (12)
Brownedge St Mary's Catholic High School, Bamber Bridge

UNTITLED

There once was a strange teenager. His mum said to get a job as he got kicked out, so he searched up jobs to do. There was a kid's party at a funfair. So he signed up.

He arrived at the party and put the clown costume on. After, the costume would not budge at all. He had to go to another party so he would have to act normal during the party. He evolved into a big clown. The police came and started to take him down. "This is not over!" Those were his last words.

Malik McGovarin (11)
Brownedge St Mary's Catholic High School, Bamber Bridge

FROZEN

Every clock had stopped. It was midday. I was on the way to meet my friends to go to the beach when all of a sudden, everything stopped. I looked to see birds just hovering in the air. I began to run, only to see cars frozen in the middle of the road. I tried to call my friend. It went straight to answerphone... I panicked, not knowing what to do... ten minutes had passed. I checked the time. I messaged my friend. Suddenly, after five minutes, a message appeared...

Chloe Robinson (12)

Brownedge St Mary's Catholic High School, Bamber Bridge

ONE LAST LIFE

"You're early," said Death, "you have three more days."
An all-black figure jumped out and it all went black. I woke up at home and got a letter. Four left.
I thought to myself, *what does that mean?*
After that, I carried on with my day like usual.
Days later, I was on my bike going to training and again a black figure struck a knife at me and everything went black. I woke up in a red room.

Joseph Cuming (12)
Brownedge St Mary's Catholic High School, Bamber Bridge

DÉJÀ VU

We buried it, but it was back. We burnt it, but it was back. We destroyed it, but it was back. The same picture from eighteen years ago was standing strong despite the many attempts to obliterate it. Was this some kind of joke? There was only one way to destroy it once and for all. Should we do it to end this nonsense or should we keep it?

Ryan Massie (12)
Brownedge St Mary's Catholic High School, Bamber Bridge

A FRESH SLATE

It was December 31st, 1999. New Year's Eve. A family were watching the countdown to the new millennium. It was 23:59, one minute away and finally, it was now the new year. But something was off. The TV and radio went quiet suddenly. Both parents dropped to the floor. Both children were freaking out and had no idea what was happening. They tried to call the police but there was no answer. They ran to a neighbour's house. They opened the door to a teenage boy. He sobbed. Both his parents had just died. He believed everyone had been cursed by a wiser power, God.

Ben Hart (14)
Cathkin High School, Cambuslang

GUILT IS A MACHINE

I know what I am. A robot with a consciousness is how they described it. But I wish I'd considered machines can malfunction. I had my blade to his throat, no control over my own body, watching his blood pool beneath him. I heard the softness of his last words, "I forgive you, I know it's not your fault." His eyes were dark, body limp, drenched in blood. "How did this happen?" I grieved. His voice echoed in my head. "I forgive you." My chest ached but I couldn't cry. He may forgive me but I will never forgive myself.

Madeleine Whyte (14)
Cathkin High School, Cambuslang

THE REFLECTION

I got dressed for school and I looked in the mirror to see if my uniform was okay. I walked off, and when I turned my head, my reflection was standing there smiling at me... I tried to scream but nothing came out. My parents dashed to my room. They saw my reflection and not theirs... They put up a new mirror and I went to bed. I woke up feeling like someone was watching me. I stood up, telling myself it was nothing. Mum shouted, "Breakfast!" I left my room and glanced back and they were back.

Carly Roberts (12)
Cathkin High School, Cambuslang

THE SUN'S REVENGE

"Everything's ready, doctor."
"Let's do this."
Suddenly, the sun was enveloped with light. The scientists looked and the sun had an eyeball. Without warning, the sun shone so bright that most humans were eradicated. On the other side of the planet, Tom Dingle, his parents and everyone else were evacuating into a cave. Then, Tom's parents, Rebecca and Jason Dingle, looked in horror as the sun started to rise. As they turned to ash, they pushed Tom into the cave. The people were then forced to eat only carrots to see in the dark caves. This was their life now.

Leo Hicks (11)
Forest Oak School, Smiths Wood

THE UNICORN CLONE

Sofia was in her room, playing with her friends, Emily and Ava. Sofia started playing a game called 'Fun, Fun, Fun'. Emily shrieked, "Don't play that game. It's dangerous." Then the power went off. Sofia was scared. Suddenly, the lights came on, and Sofia saw Ava holding a unicorn in her hand.

"Why is there a unicorn in my hand? Where is Emily?"

"Ava, Sofia, it's me."

"Did it just talk?" said Ava and Sofia.

"You bread loaf."

She magically turned back. How strange was that?

Serenity Whyte (12)
Forest Oak School, Smiths Wood

ENTER IF YOU DARE

Rose and Ragaya were in Rose's room, playing on their phones. Ragaya told Rose about an app that was forbidden. It was called 'Enter If You Dare'. Rose thought it sounded good, so she downloaded the app.

Suddenly, the girls realised they had disappeared from the room and were in a dark limo. They were really scared. Darkness surrounded the limo, and the limo kept driving on its own. They kept on trying the doors, but they did not work. This became their life, travelling in the forever-driving limo. If only they hadn't opened the app!

Scarlett Dyke (12)
Forest Oak School, Smiths Wood

THE MAGICAL LAND

Libby loved to read books, and her favourite place was the library. One day, when she was choosing some books, she spotted a secret door. She opened it and came into a magical land. There were lots of creatures like werewolves. She was scared, but she had some meat, so they became friends. When it was time for her to go back home, she turned to go back through the magical door, but it would not open! The werewolves decided to turn her into a werewolf and she stayed in the magical land forever.

Aaliyah Gourlay (11)
Forest Oak School, Smiths Wood

THE STRANGE LIFT

Dan was in a shop, so he got into a lift. Suddenly, he felt the lift going down. The lift stopped. He was in a labyrinth. If he wanted to leave, he would have to escape the labyrinth. He heard a noise to his left and his right. It was a growl. He was scared. He needed to get back to the lift! Fifty years went on, and he still hadn't found the lift. His life was hiding from the growl and looking for the lift.

William Powers (11)
Forest Oak School, Smiths Wood

THE TIME MACHINE

I was making my time machine in my room when all of a sudden, my time machine broke. I went back in time fifteen million years. Then I lost the time machine. *Now I'm stuck here...* I found the materials to build a new time machine. I just needed to find one more item to get back to the present, but unfortunately, what I needed was in the present.

Jack Salmon (11)
Forest Oak School, Smiths Wood

RECONSTELLATION

Have you ever woken at night, where half your bedroom has disintegrated, with Fate knocking at your window? Because that's what happened to me. Fate boomed, "People's stars have been mismatched. Only you can return them."
"Why me?"
"Your memory is photographic and you believe in magic. You have telekinesis."
Fate vanished.
People were screaming as roads gradually withered away. It all made sense: if people didn't have destinies, then what was life's essence? I looked at the sky. Orion's Belt resembled a sword. Summoning my telekinesis, I rearranged the constellations, making the world normal. Who mismatched destiny to begin with?

Sharon Kenneth (11)
King Edward VI Five Ways School, Bartley Green

THE GLITCH

Once, planets were ruled by the controller. He had a game called 'Earth'.

One day, the game 'Earth' started glitching; the characters inside suffered the most.

Inside the game, people were disappearing randomly - at lunch, schooltime, bedtime - it was chaos.

The President was giving a speech about these mysterious events and then he vanished, leaving weird computer codings.

The controller saw this and thought the game was rusty. His assistant checked it out.

"The game will have to go."

"But the characters."

"Do it! Now!"

The controller unplugged Earth and on Planet Earth, humans saw a meteor crashing down.

Freya Coombe
King Edward VI Five Ways School, Bartley Green

JOURNEY ACROSS THE WORLDS

Once, long ago, there was nothing. Then came an orb, then life. Seeing the orb, they worshipped it and built it a shrine to guard it. But one day, a man tried to steal it but failed. The people decided to inhabit planets created by the orb and some stayed cursed with immortality. Twenty million years later.

"AOAO!"

"What, Z1R2? I'm busy!"

"Come."

They left the meeting room and went to the orb.

"It's glitching and you know what could happen... Ah, X2A5, tell us something."

"The stability is low and a portal could open soon..."

Flash! A portal opened...

Reuben Singh Sangera Punia (12)

King Edward VI Five Ways School, Bartley Green

BINARY BIOTECHNICIANS

"No... No!" I collapsed, being eradicated from the software by the second. 0s and 1s surrounded me. Now, the hacker chiefs had official authority because of me, Luca. But unusually, they continued typing relentlessly. I'd accepted my fate. *Zwoop!* The colosseum travelled time and the firewall destabilised. Silence. Then, my body dispersed in countless realities, like food being ripped apart, but eventually chose one. They had hacked me - or so I thought. It felt like a movie. I spotted a hacker master that looked like me but... different.

"My name is Acu-L," he said, "and the countdown has begun..."

Joseph Mukoro (11)
King Edward VI Five Ways School, Bartley Green

THE GLITCH

Hester sat outside an old, dilapidated shop her ringlets drenched and straightened from the rain. She had searched for shelter to no avail.

Ophelia was delivering her final parcel to the daughter of the obsidian king in the Thyxill Layer.

Suddenly, a thunderous scream shattered the layer, removing all magical protections. Destiny's book, containing the fate of every individual, was missing.

The book fell heavily at Hester's feet with a loud thud. When she opened it to find her page, she discovered a curse placed on her bloodline.

Although devastated, Hester decided to confront Destiny with courage and determination.

Janani Kumara Gurubaran
King Edward VI Five Ways School, Bartley Green

THE GLITCH

Hans sprinted through the dim alley, pressed against the cold brick. Echoes of glitches pursued him relentlessly, prompting him to confront the power he loathed. Donning the headset, unlike others, he didn't glitch, but gained speed, strength, and the uncanny ability to phase through walls. Relentlessly embracing his newfound gift, he aimed to dismantle the Glitch Corps, the creator of the ominous headset. At the heart of the chase, he confronted the imposing structure - Glitch Corps, a fortress of security and a harbour of the technological menace threatening to consume him. Hans stood determined, ready to unravel the mystery within.

Khaleeq Badmus (12)
King Edward VI Five Ways School, Bartley Green

THE LOOP BEGINS

In a quiet town, whispers of 'the glitch' circulated like an unsettling breeze. Jacq, a curious teenager, stumbled upon an old PlayStation. He booted it up and got sucked into it, leaving the real world behind. Inside the game, he was chased by a terrifying monster who wanted to kill him. Suddenly, he turned around to see the monster transforming into an older version of himself. "What?" he exclaimed. "Stay away from me!"

The clone shouted, "Come with me, I can help you to escape this hellish place."

So Jacq followed him, jumping from game to game and from dimension to dimension.

Daniyel Oche (12)

King Edward VI Five Ways School, Bartley Green

ROKUROKUBI

Crack. The rips on the screen of the console opened up like an abyss. Mysterious substances leaked from the crevices. My walls started to compact, suffocating me. The room slowly became pixelated. I awoke in an ancient library. Thick dust flooded the shelves. Intrigued, I strolled through twisted hallways despite the cold penetrating through me. I stopped in my tracks. A girl sneered at me. My heart pounded. I could hear my breath. Suddenly, her neck stretched towards me. Was I hallucinating? Then it hit me; it was her, Rokurokubi.
She snickered, "Finally figured it out?"

Ellen Cheng
King Edward VI Five Ways School, Bartley Green

THE GLITCH

"You're early," said Death, "What happened...?"
It was her and her brother. They had to fend for themselves.
Their parents had gone ten years ago. That glitchy AI made
so many buildings fall. Made so many people lose their lives.
The siblings stole from shops and slept on a bed of rubble.
They had been like this for ten years. As the tenth year
came, a collapsing building separated them. The girl had to
carry on. She saw another and ran towards him. They fell in
love. They rebuilt the world together. After, her brother
watched, smiling from Heaven with Death.

Shania Dadrah (12)
King Edward VI Five Ways School, Bartley Green

THE LOOP

Objects started floating in the sky. I ran into my house.
"Jacq!"
The Glitch called my name. I grabbed an apple and ran. I saw my PlayStation was broken. Good riddance!
I ran and ran and hid behind a rock and ate my apple. It tasted really good.
However, that was my mistake. The Glitch had found me. I was horrified!
I saw my dad inside the monster. Even though I was shocked, I still kept on running.
I ran and ran until it caught up and touched me. I started turning glitchy. Not again.
The loop had restarted again!

Shaurya Iyengar (11)
King Edward VI Five Ways School, Bartley Green

THE GLITCH

There was once an alien called Zain. Zain was a quiet young boy in a quiet school. It was perfect for Zain. However, sometimes Zain would feel lonely because he had no friends. Every day, Zain would sit on the bench all alone and would sometimes get bullied for being a 'bookworm'. That was his nickname. They were the same boys that Zain would think, *I wish I was just like them.* But would Zain's life stay as it was, or would it alter after Zain stood up for himself...?

Hyabel Ukbit (12)
King Edward VI Five Ways School, Bartley Green

THE BOY WHO MET DEATH

"You're early," said Death.

"What happened?" asked Ben.

"You're dead - well, nearly dead, I suppose. The only thing that's keeping you alive is the ICU unit you're in right now," replied Death.

"Hang on. That's not fair! The last thing I remember doing was putting my hair dryer in my bathtub to warm up the water, and then I appeared here," exclaimed Ben.

"Yeah, you electrocuted yourself," replied Death. "However, there is one way I can allow you to live."

"Yes, yes! What is it?" asked Ben.

"You have to let someone dear to you take your place."

Samihuz Zaman (14)
London East Academy, London

CANVAS OF DESTINY

Alexander entered a dilapidated museum in the heart of Venice. The building was constructed during the Enlightenment and was later purchased by an old billionaire who turned it into a museum. Wandering through corridors adorned with paintings that shared untold secrets of time, Alexander stumbled upon a peculiar painting that depicted a destroyed cityscape. Almost everything was completely annihilated except for a tower in the middle of the city. The strangest thing was that at the very edge of the painting, there was a Latin inscription that said,
"It happened once, and it will happen again. Find me and save yourself."

Mahir Rahman (14)
London East Academy, London

MAX'S GLITCH

The sun hadn't risen for five years. It was the year 2184, casting the world into a permanent twilight. In this reality, Max, a skilled programmer, stumbled upon a mysterious glitch in the stimulated sky. Max undercovered an anomaly that held the key to the sun's prolonged absence. As they manipulated the digital threads, an unexpected surge of light burst forth, blurring the boundaries between the virtual and real. Max's creation glitched, birthing an artificial sunrise that painted the horizon with hues unseen for half a decade. The glitch became a beacon of hope, bringing a small sense of hope.

Fhahad Ahmed (14)
London East Academy, London

A SHOCK FROM THE FUTURE

Ignoring the warnings, he downloaded the app. As soon as his finger touched the button, everything disappeared into a swirly haze of many different colours. As it disappeared from his sight, his eyes adjusted to the bright lights of the new scenes unfolding before his eyes. As he looked around, his eyes grew bigger with each sight he took in. From flying cars to robots cleaning the streets and delivering packages, it was just like the app which he downloaded on his phone. Suddenly, he heard a loud beep from behind him. Before he could react, he fell down, stunned...

Muhammad Alom (13)
London East Academy, London

THE DAY WITH NO NIGHT

Sunrise. People from all over the world began their day as normal, unaware of the fact that it would never end. At exactly 12pm Greenwich Mean Time, the entire universe and everything to do with time just *stopped*. Just like in the movies. The British had noon, the Americans had morning, the West Asians had sunset, and the East Asians and Australians had night. And so it was to be for the rest of eternity. Millions died across the world within weeks, but Seth Rodgerman would not be like them. People hid, people burrowed, but Seth's time machine departed.

Yahya Kasoma (14)
London East Academy, London

THE INVASION

Once upon a time, there was a village. It was a happy place until a voice came out of the village speaker.
It said, "I will come for you."
The villagers got scared and went to Zen for help. He told the villagers not to worry; he would take care of it. He waited until he thought he could defeat Destroyer.
Suddenly, Destroyer came. Zen intercepted Destroyer, and they started to battle, and there were loud sounds of metal on metal. When it finished, Destroyer surrendered, and Zen had won. Thankfully, the villagers made Zen king of the village.

Riyad Dahbi (13)
London East Academy, London

THE CONTROLLING CON AND RUN

Ignoring the warnings, I downloaded the app. I heard rumours spreading that an app was controlling people. Being curious, I installed it. The app had a blue icon. I opened it and a charming and eloquent voice began speaking to me. As it spoke, a feeling was intensifying within me. I tried to close the app, but I couldn't and realised that I had succumbed to my own curiosity. The feeling was beginning to spread throughout my body. It reached my heart, then my brain. As I was mindlessly staring at the screen, some text appeared. I was given a first task.

Awwab Ibne-Razi (15)
London East Academy, London

UNTITLED

Every clock in the world had stopped. It seemed as if I was stuck in a multidimensional universe. Everyone around me was frozen except for one unexpected individual. Mr Jones. The old man who lived across the street. Something was definitely wrong and he must be part of it. I sneaked around behind the wall and watched him. He pulled out a purple block from his pocket and tapped it twice. It seemed to have summoned a portal. The perfect size for a human. Before he stepped into it, he looked directly into my eyes, as though he had supervision...

Yahyaa Abdur Rahman (14)
London East Academy, London

OPERATION SISTER GONE WRONG

When Claire was small she always wanted a sister, but her mum wasn't willing to. Years later, Claire worked at a tech company, and one day they made an invention that could clone anything. She heard this and thought she could finally have a sister so she snuck in at midnight and went in the machine but something went wrong and the whole thing blew up, with her inside it. Later, scientists came and said there was a glitch that caused the explosion. Her body wasn't found, and they discovered she was in another dimension with no way out.

Umar Mirza (13)
London East Academy, London

THE EFFEREM SYNDICATE

Day and night blended without any celestial objects. It didn't help that we were in prison, but today, that would change. We'd saved up from our work each day, buying only necessary food to enter the conclave. This was a black market within the prison, where we had brought our gear. We'd been preparing for too long, and now it was time to strike. We made short work of the gate with wire cutters from the conclave. I didn't enjoy having to stab a guard, but I had something to think about while I was asleep in another prison.

Ibraheem Hussain (13)
London East Academy, London

THE FIGURE

The night fell, covering the town in a thick blanket. The streets were barren without a soul in sight. No cars. No people. Nothing. A crow was the only living species to be seen. A towering, decrepit lamp post stood there. It began to flicker, and then the spirit had left. The street was lifeless. It was pitch-dark. A cold absence travelled with the wind. A figure was noticed in the distance. It came closer. The figure was tall and skinny. I panicked. The figure was at arm's length. I ran. It followed me. I stopped. Blood gushed...

Ayaan Ahmed (13)
London East Academy, London

DIED TOO SOON

"You're early," said Death. "What happened?"

Ophelia smiled. "I need my sister."

Death sighed. "Vampires were May's end. Suicide wasn't supposed to be yours. You upset the natural order." Death continued, "I should revive you, you know."

"Don't," Ophelia pleaded.

"Only if you accept my offer."

"Anything."

"You stay dead, but May comes back."

"Done," Ophelia said abruptly.

"Are you sure, love?" Death asked. Ophelia nodded. Death sighed and opened the gates.

"Thank you," whispered Ophelia and she stepped into the light with a smile. The gates closed.

"I'll never understand mortals' love for one another," Death murmured and sighed.

Isabella Hollingsworth (13)

Queen Katharine Academy, Walton

A WORLD OF CHAOS

"Bacon, do you know why you're here?"

"N-no..."

"Well - robots, get him!"

"No!" Bacon sprinted off into the hall. He knew where to go - the toilet - to quickly fart! But then, he got hit by a bomb.

"Welcome to Heaven - argh! You stink! Go to hell, stinky," Spongebob cried. Bacon watched as he fell over.

"Welcome to - Argh! You foul-smelling poop! Go and take a shower!" Satan instructed. Bacon did as he said, rose from the dead, and went home to take a shower! *What a day!* Bacon thought.

"Bacon! Cheese for dinner? Come down!" Grandma shouted.

Dylan Murphy (11)
Queen Katharine Academy, Walton

SPIDER-MAN AND SPIDERBOY

One day, there were two friends living in New York City. When Peter was having a shower, he screamed so loudly that it woke the whole of 5th Avenue up, so Kieran went upstairs to ask,

"What happened?"

Peter said, "I think I got bitten by a spider!"

"Oh," Kieran said.

"Argh!" Kieran said loudly, "I think I got bitten as well by the same spider."

Then Peter said, "Let's see if we have spider powers."

"Yeah!" Kieran said loudly.

Then they went outside, and finally, they had spider powers, so they were named Spider-Man and Spiderboy.

Kieran Hurdman (13)

Queen Katharine Academy, Walton

A HOMELESS GIRL CALLED MATILDA

Once upon a time, there was a little girl who was homeless and a lady looked at her and said to her, "Are you okay and what's your name honey?"

She said, "I am homeless and my name is Matilda."

She said, "Oh, you would like a home and some warm clothes. This is your new home. It is like a white, black mansion."

She said, "Are you rich?"

"Yes, I am Matilda."

"What is your name?"

"Honey, Miss Honey."

"Hello, Miss Honey. Can you be my mom, please? And you are beautiful, loving, gentle, like a koala hugging me in my hands."

Masey Long (12)
Queen Katharine Academy, Walton

THE ANCIENT REVIVAL

Humans are cooperating with the gods to prevent extinction. The gods are buzzing about, doing the 'inevitable' thing. Reviving the dead from the Underworld: Hades' Realm. Everyone is helping to convince Hades and Mother Nature. All the multiverses have clashed: Harry Potter, Twilight, you name it! The government has finally intervened. Things are going back to normal, as normal as it was in Gen Z. But youngsters are rare... unless there was a glitch - during which everyone was youthful. But that can't be, right? Could Gaia be plotting revenge against the world for killing Kronos? None knows! As they shouldn't...

Edlin Elsa Edison (12)
Queen Katharine Academy, Walton

THE DRAWINGS

The drawings predicted the future.

I walked through the museum, looking at each image. There were pictures for each historical event, one year before it started. The brick wall was completely covered.

In the corner, a frail old lady sat with a sketchpad. As I approached, I asked, "What are you drawing?" I could see her past pictures. February 17th, 2024 - exactly one year ago today. There were explosions everywhere, people dying. That's when I heard it. Sirens, explosions, screams. Bombs broke the museum ceiling. I screamed.

Bang!

I collapsed, my whole body going numb. I was dead.

Neelah Springthorpe (13)
Queen Katharine Academy, Walton

ICE-COLD WASTELAND

It was 3585, and we were the most advanced country, well the only country. My country's name was New Pangice. We got the name from the old continent in the Jurassic period. Well, anyway, our technology was so advanced, we have everything you could ever think of. It was a peaceful life until it wasn't...

In that year, a star called Glisa-667 passed through our solar system and rained meteors at us. One-quarter of the population died, but the rest survived. But it isn't over...

After the shower of meteors, we got kicked out of our solar system and now we need to survive in a barren wasteland.

Yenara Madanayaka (13)
Queen Katharine Academy, Walton

LET ME IN

"The party sounds fun, doesn't it?" I said to my mate, Gregory.

"Yes, it does! Am I dressed okay?" he asked.

"There's going to be drinks!" I shouted.

But, outside the house, a shiver ran deep down my spine. This wasn't a normal house. Two people emerged from the house and dragged me and Gregory in. One told me to sit down in front of an 'ordinary' ball. Gregory sat beside me.

"Tell it you allow them in," a voice said. Fear made me say it.

"I allow you in. We allow you in."

"Who? No... What's that...?"

Bella Marshall (13)
Queen Katharine Academy, Walton

THE CURE

I sprinted through the lab, Claire beside me. My ears were ringing. The screeches of the zombies didn't help. I hadn't realised Claire had turned a corner. I had been so lost in thought. We were looking for Damon, the scientist who helped us escape the lab, since he said I was 'the cure', or something. Cure for what though? A zombie pulled my leg. However, someone stabbed its back. Damon. I mumbled a thanks as we ran.

"Run, Valerie!" I stared at him in surprise as he stopped running.

"You can save the zombies. You're the cure, Valerie."

"Cure?"

Kaci Marriott (12)
Queen Katharine Academy, Walton

THE DARKEST ATTACK

The sun hadn't risen for a whole week. Then, we knew. People flying, humans attacking each other. Well, we thought they were human. They weren't.

Finally, the sun rose again. The flying men disintegrated. The attacks stopped. Until the next day.

It all started again, but this time people died and others rushed to hospital. The flying men had wolf-like fangs and ate human flesh, dropping clumps onto our heads. These men weren't human. They were flesh-eating vampires!

They took over the world and ate all of humankind. We were forced into hiding, and to never leave our own homes.

Destiny Price (12)
Queen Katharine Academy, Walton

PAUSE

I was bored. Fiddling with the stop button on the remote, I decided to go outside.
Wandering down the street, cold sweat trickled down my neck. People were standing everywhere I looked. They were still; it was as if somebody had paused them. I was trembling, panic-stricken. It was soundless. The only sound was my own breath. The people were staring at me like silent sentries. I was speechless. I didn't know what to do. Just then, glacial, spine-tingling hands swiped across my exposed shoulders. Goosebumps appeared all over my body. I was frightened. I stood still, like everyone else.

Juta Butvydaite (12)
Queen Katharine Academy, Walton

ELECTRONIC DISCOVERY

Ever since the atomic bomb in 2023, the USA has suffered tremendously and beyond repair. Nova was a new archaeologist assigned to excavate an abandoned nuclear plant.

As she stepped inside, she smelt the radiation and dust. Unaware of the lurking troubles, she started clearing the place of troublesome items. When Nova picked up a hand-held computer with a large red button, the room fell black. Fear choked her like hands tightening on her neck. Accidentally, she pressed the button, leading to a loud alarm sound and a green, burning liquid filling the room. *Bang!* She fainted.

Vanessa Sketrys (11)
Queen Katharine Academy, Walton

WHAT IF MONEY DID NOT EXIST?

"If money wasn't an object what would the world be like?"
I was looking up to the sky and seeing a busy town in the reflection of the glass skyscrapers.
"If we started with no money what would it be like if we never had it?"
A boy bumped into me, "What is this money stuff you're talking about?"
I kept looking up before I replied that I didn't know. Then I realised what I said had come true. Money never had existed to him... so how do *I* know that it did?
So now I'm going to find out how this all happened.

Amelia-Mai Crick (13)
Queen Katharine Academy, Walton

KALIFA THE ALIEN AND THE GREAT MUSHROOM

One day, Kalifa and her sister were riding their bikes to school when all of a sudden a great storm formed in the clouds out of nowhere. It made a gigantic massive colossol ring above the clouds.

Then the force of gravity pulled Kaifa and her sister up into the clouds through another dimension. Suddenly a strange alien gave them a hand and pulled both of them into the clouds.

"Well, hello there dear child," said the mushroom.

"Why are we here? Where are we?" Kalifa said as her sister screamed.

"You'll see..." said the mushroom.

Mia Njeru (12)
Queen Katharine Academy, Walton

THE DIGITAL WAR

Back when the Soviets and the USA had a space race, a collision happened on the moon and the planets were never seen again. It affected the world beyond repair and left Earth as a toxic wasteland. Florence stared at the blank sky. She was a Russian prisoner of war and was used to hack into the Russian confidential websites.

"Oi, come on, will ya!" the guard screamed.

Florence limped into the computer room, sitting in her personal seat and revealing their secrets. However, there was one detrimental thing. It could affect mankind and even the entire planet.

Vanessa Sketrys (11)
Queen Katharine Academy, Walton

ONE MYSTERY DAY

Every clock had stopped, except for one - the one in my classroom.

All of the lights turned off and on, flickering non-stop.

Something was happening. The ground was shaking, everyone was shouting, screaming, "Help!"

Next thing, my arm was itchy and there was writing on it saying, "You have been granted a superpower. Every time you click your fingers, you will make the Earth move. Also, if you click your fingers twice, it will stop moving around and up and down."

I clicked my fingers twice and all of a sudden, we were back to normal!

Callum Baylis (13)
Queen Katharine Academy, Walton

WHAT IF ALL THE CHILDREN TURNED INTO FRANKENSTEIN MONSTERS?

Gloomy clouds drifted away as parents and children slept tight. All of a sudden, rain pounded upon the windows of children's bedrooms, waking them with a fright.

All of the children's skin started changing into a vomit-like, green colour, and their eyes began to grow larger and larger as if they were making room for the bolts that began to grow into them. They just froze in place as sweat began to trickle down their foreheads. The parents had yet to see to their children, who had mysteriously changed overnight. What or who was behind all of this mystery?

Khadija Ahmed (12)
Queen Katharine Academy, Walton

THE VIRUS OF MISERY

Once, there was a group of kids who were trapped by Wicked. Thomas, Newt, Minho, Frypan and Gally had an unexpected guest. A girl in a boy's only glade. Her name was Teresa, and she arrived knowing Thomas' name. All eyes had landed on Thomas. Everyone started questioning him.

She had a note in her hand. "She's the last one ever," Newt had read. Everyone escaped the maze and arrived at the last city without knowing anything. Newt had the virus. Thomas tried his best to save him, but it was too late. Newt had become a Crank. Everyone said goodbye.

Arfa Naveed (11)
Queen Katharine Academy, Walton

THE DRAWING PREDICTED THE FUTURE!

Poppy would be drawing all the time. She went to Hampton Primary School. Her friends were Lilly, Mike and Josh. They were on their way to school when they came upon a spaceship. They all had on a shocked face. Poppy was obviously still drawing during that moment. While they were walking to school, Josh noticed Poppy drawing a spaceship. The next minute, they came upon a spaceship. John thought, *could she see the future?* Poppy also drew them all inside of the spaceship. They all went into the spaceship and found about ten aliens, all looking weird at them all.

Macey Mueller (11)
Queen Katharine Academy, Walton

THE MOMENT IT ALL CHANGED

"You're early, what happened?"
Six years ago my sister died, and then everything changed, it got dark very, very early. The sun rose very late in the day. The sun started rising at midday, and it was very unusual. Wolves came out during the day at exactly 1pm, it was so strange and weird. But then something else happened, all my family members gathered up for a pep talk, it was the 22nd of August at this moment, at 8am. At night they would all gather up and practise their fighting skills which I thought was awkward, but then, they tried to kill me.

Jessie Stanley (11)
Queen Katharine Academy, Walton

PARALLEL GRANDMA

Why did it happen again? Why was I transferred into a new universe again? But this one was different. My dead grandma was alive, but she wasn't at the same time. You could see bits of her skull. She had only one arm and her eyes were glowing red.

She stared at me and said, "It's breakfast time," with a deep voice.

She started walking over to me. It was as if she wanted me for breakfast. She ran straight at me. Quickly, I felt queasy and unwell.

"Now, you have joined me, my grandson," she said.

I fell, fearfully.

Theo Hollingsworth (11)
Queen Katharine Academy, Walton

THE GIRL WHO TRIED TO HURT THE COUNTRY

The sun hadn't risen for five years until, one day, a girl came to the country. Once she got settled in, she somehow made the sky have a sun again. Everyone hated her, so they made a plan to take her away. People started getting angry, so they finally carried out the plan.

"Go away. We don't want you here," everyone screamed.

The next day, she ran away because of what everybody said to her. They lived happily ever after and carried on with their lives.

But suddenly, something happened. No one knew what, so everyone went away.

Lilly-Rose Beeny (14)
Queen Katharine Academy, Walton

THE GLITCHED DOLL

For my daughter's birthday, I gifted her a doll. She had always wanted one! One night I heard a loud scream, I sprinted to my daughter's room... but she was fast asleep! I was utterly confused. Looking around, I saw the doll, its mechanical mouth wide open. I grabbed the weird doll and buried it in my front garden. I hoped that my daughter wouldn't notice its disappearance, but of course she did. I told her it probably got lost.

That night, I went into my daughter's bright pink room and looked at her, she was holding the doll I buried...

Mia Merrison (11)

Queen Katharine Academy, Walton

THE GLITCH

It all started on the 14th of August 2010 on a plane ride to Egypt. It was a smooth ride until it wasn't. Suddenly, the plane started to head downwards, and everyone started to panic. Without warning, everything went black. After what seemed like forever, I woke up. Everybody was dead except me.

I went outside. We had crashed into a jungle. I went to explore, and I stopped in front of a river. I didn't move, but my reflection did. Behind me, I saw something. A spooky creature limped towards me. I was terrified. My life flashed before my eyes...

Muskaan Shanzad (12)
Queen Katharine Academy, Walton

THE MIDNIGHT WALK

The wind whistled as Nalla opened her door for her midnight walk. She decided to take a new trail this time. Instead of her usual way, she went through the forest. Nalla made her way down the dark forest, enjoying the breeze that flowed through her dark, black, glossy hair. She stopped for a second and closed her eyes, listening to the owls hoot and the foxes scavenging around her, until she heard a loud thud and a horrifying scream. Nalla's eyes widened in shock, looking around, worried and terrified, until she turned around and saw a man. A vampire...

Olivia Feerick (12)
Queen Katharine Academy, Walton

JEALOUS JENNA AND A BAT

It was a snowy night for Jack. He was just about to finish baking and all of a sudden his girlfriend Jenna called him and asked, in a polite voice, "Do you want to come over and spend time with me?"

Jack said, "Yeah, sure!"

"I'll meet you outside my front door. Bye!"

"Alright," said Jack. He walked down the stairs and smiled in excitement.

Jack walked inside the house and there was no sight of Jenna. He walked around the whole house but there was still no Jenna. Suddenly Jack dropped down...

Mario Tambura (12)
Queen Katharine Academy, Walton

RADIO OF REVOLUTION

The radio was charred and burning, yet it was still playing. The grass was grey and there was silence apart from the flames burning.

The revolution broke out two years previously. Could half of humanity have been wiped out?

All track of humanity had been lost and the destruction was irreparable. It spread like a disease. Everywhere were signs of destruction. The world was blackened.

Then the radio stopped playing. An ear-wrenching static came out. The charred radio crumbled to pieces. The static stopped, but the radio continued playing...

Antoni Mikucki (11)
Queen Katharine Academy, Walton

EVERYONE IS GONE

It was a normal day; well that's what I thought. Arriving at science, I set my bag by the window, grabbed my pen and sat down.

I sat down, but I started to feel light-headed. I rocked side to side. Suddenly, there was a loud *thump!* Everything went black and silent.

"Sarah, Sarah, wake up!" exclaimed a distant voice.

I saw a bunch of lines and shapes as if it was a glitch. Everything zoomed out and I snapped back to reality, but something was odd. Everyone had disappeared. It was the glitch they had warned me about.

Lilly Faull (12)
Queen Katharine Academy, Walton

I DIDN'T MOVE BUT MY REFLECTION DID

Amelia moved to London and went to a new school. She went to the toilets and looked at her reflection in the mirror. As she looked closer to the mirror, she realised that her reflection was moving when she wasn't!

She found it very creepy and even strange. Every time she would go to the toilets or towards a mirror that showed her reflection, she started seeing even creepier things like her reflection communicating with her.

Eventually, things got even weirder as she saw her reflection speaking to an actual person who wasn't herself.

Kotryna Krutkeviciute (13)
Queen Katharine Academy, Walton

UNTITLED

Today is the last time the sun will arise itself on the Earth. Every one hundred years, the sun will release a fraction of its power to engulf the Earth in flames of fire. My name is John and today's solar storms have been unstable lately. This might be my last recording. The world has been under a purge ever since the government revealed the truth about the world and the prophecy of the stars aligning with each other. Some people can't accept the end. Others, however, would just make the time for the most. The sky is red. Our death prevails.

Jayden Ross Santos De Sesto (13)
Queen Katharine Academy, Walton

THE LONELY GIRL

She walked through the forest alone, barefoot with her red polka dot dress which looked like it had been ripped by a wild animal.
She had a very good twin sister who was always favoured by their parents. She was very jealous of her sister because she would get all the attention. Maria was seen as the evil sister and Evie was seen as the good sister.
Maria decided to run away because she felt invisible.
A couple of days went by and she decided to go home. As she rang the doorbell, her mum looked at her confused. Was she real?

Zeinib Rahi (13)
Queen Katharine Academy, Walton

THE ORDINARY BOY WITH EXTRAORDINARY POWERS

One day, there was a little boy who found out he was magical. He started off as an ordinary boy but then discovered he could do stuff other people couldn't. "Mum, look! I can make this float!" said Jake. Little things like books, water, or anything really, he could make float and move them side to side or spill liquids, smash glass or bang rocks. His mum got him checked at the doctor's to see if it was just him with the powers, but it wasn't normal. Only two percent of people have the ability to do it and Jack was one...

Aniyah Rehman (11)
Queen Katharine Academy, Walton

CAT KID

There was an ordinary kid called Peter. A radioactive cat bit him when he went on his trampoline. He jumped over his house and landed on the right. He had night vision. He made a costume and became Cat Kid. He went through the night helping people and kicking villains, but one day, when he was walking, he heard something. A mouse was there; it was Mouse Man. He transformed into his human form. "Now die," he exclaimed.

Cat Kid jumped out of his log. He kicked and used his scratch, and then it happened: a new power-up came.

Daniel Sousa Loly (11)
Queen Katharine Academy, Walton

UNTITLED

Sarah goes to Winter Wonderland and meets her friends there, called Liam, Sheila, Eva, Patricia, and Eric. They all meet up. They find people they hate. They call them over and say to them, "Let's go get food."
They go get food and then they go near all the grass and kill them, and then bury them. Then some of her friends get chased. Sarah tries finding them, but they are nowhere to be seen, but she keeps looking for them. She finds them eventually. The people didn't die. Sarah finds them digging out of their graves...

Shania Hogan (12)
Queen Katharine Academy, Walton

NIGHTMARES

I was dressed and ready to sleep. Suddenly, the light went out. I was all alone in the dark room. I decided to sleep straight away. I heard a sound down in the kitchen. It started raining. I went downstairs. Something was moving. It was all dressed in black. Something grabbed me. I was screaming, trying to escape. It said, "Guys, come on, I have found dinner." I saw more black things all dressed in black. They all started climbing on me. I saw the leader; much bigger. It jumped on me. I screamed. I found out it was all a nightmare.

Jemima Adegunna (13)
Queen Katharine Academy, Walton

THE MISSING GIRL

Ignoring the warnings, Anabelle downloaded the app. Little did she know, her life was about to change. The app had access to all her private information and her location.
One day, when Anabelle was walking to the shop, a man started to follow her. The man knew who she was as he had access to all her information. The man took her from the side of the road and she never returned. Her parents were worried and called the police as she hadn't returned. The police had been searching for two years and they are still searching to this day.

Alayna Ahmed (11)
Queen Katharine Academy, Walton

INTERGALACTIC WAR

I was on the floor, my gear and helmet broken on the battlefield. I was fighting for Lord Maria. This war began five years ago. The two queens of the galaxy had a falling out. Maria and Lena were inseparable but then Lena committed a cruel crime. The galaxy split in three. The Marias, the Lenas and the Neutrals.
I'm in Maria's army. The second I was born I joined this fight. Bloodshed, violence and war are a part of me. Life isn't worth living. The second you're born, you might as well be dead. I just got lucky. Almost.

Annabelle Skingsley (12)
Queen Katharine Academy, Walton

MAFIA WORLD

Lee, Mark and his partners want to murder a guy named Taeyong. Taeyong and Mark's family are enemies. They want to murder each other. Mark has planned something in the future to get rid of Taeyong and his mates. Eventually, they meet up to kill each other. A guy named Yuta, who is on Mark's team, gets shot by one of Taeyong's mates and that's when Mark loses his patience and shoots Taeyong, but Taeyong is not that easy to kill. They attack each other but Taeyong and his mates run away as fast as they can but then Mark...

Safah Islam (13)
Queen Katharine Academy, Walton

THE GREEN THINGS ARE COMING

The sun hadn't risen for five years. I was really scared, but just today it rose, and the world went into lockdown. All my friends and family were scared, but I ignored the warnings and went outside. As my feet touched the ground it became dark again, so I looked up and saw a really big spaceship with green men jumping down. At first, I thought they were friendly but I soon realised that they had guns pointing down at me. As my family were searching for me I screamed in pain as the green things shot me, but I am still so confused.

Harry Roddis (12)
Queen Katharine Academy, Walton

HOW I MET MY BEST FRIEND!

One cold, gloomy night, I was woken up by a loud bang. I checked outside my window and it was this long, thin-looking thing! I rushed downstairs and went through the door to see an alien standing right in front of me. I slowly walked towards it and it started talking weirdly. It was like it was talking in a different language! It told me her name was Tiffany. I said we should become friends and Tiffany agreed. The next morning, she came to my house again and we became best friends after hanging out with each other every single day.

Maizie Howley-Burke (13)
Queen Katharine Academy, Walton

THE CLOCK

Every clock had stopped. It was a sunny morning but nothing was moving, except me.

I pondered on why no one or nothing was moving. I went to my friend's house, thinking she did all this. But no, someone had stopped a clock, making every clock stop. I tried to move every clock back, but that one clock kept stopping, so I had to break it.

I travelled back in time, so I ran to the house (where the person stopped time) and tried to stop him. He didn't listen to me, so I grabbed his arm and stopped. To be continued...

Emily French (11)
Queen Katharine Academy, Walton

ALCOHOLIC FATHER

We buried it, but it came back...
One day, I was teleporting around until something stopped me. It was my dead father stopping me from going further. I could've sworn I had buried him long ago. I tried to hit him for all he'd done to me as a child, and... it worked. He was on the floor in a matter of seconds, and I went to bury him again. I carried on teleporting around my neighbourhood and stopping people from doing things they would regret. My dead dad was an alcoholic. What if my dad never arose from his grave?

Dovidas Grigor Jevas (12)
Queen Katharine Academy, Walton

BEHIND YOU IT STANDS, WATCHING

I didn't move but my reflection did...

In the early summer, I bought a mirror from the local shop called 'Glitch'. The mirror's reflection had a 3D look and dazed me with surprise because it moved! I didn't even know how.

I brought it back to my house. Time passed and I wanted to sleep. Well, I wish I had because I made a big mistake. I'd gone to get a glass of hot milk when I stared at the mirror and the glass started to crack and bleed and nothing was in it. But, behind me, it stood watching.

Logan Harradine (12)
Queen Katharine Academy, Walton

SNAKES TRYING TO TAKE OVER

In the deep, dark woods, there were snakes upon snakes and there was a walkway for people to walk through.
One day, a person walked through and the snakes were hungry and then slithering at the woman. Then she flew into the air but when she was going up, the snakes struck but just slightly missed and more snakes came but this woman's superpowers were amazing. The snakes could not do anything to eat and kill her. What if she did get bitten by the snakes? Would she die or come back to life? Her superpowers are unknown.

Harry Boyce (11)
Queen Katharine Academy, Walton

THE DISAPPEARANCE

"Every clock had stopped." It was a weird day that I will never forget. It all started on a rainy day in Memphis, Tennessee, it was dead silent. For some reason, there was no one.
It was all covered in plants. I checked the news and saw that everyone in Memphis had randomly disappeared but only when it was dark did I hear the sound of everybody all around.
I was shocked, I rubbed my eyes and it turned out I was dreaming. It was empty and all the clocks were still frozen on the same time. 12:15am, Monday.

Michael Cavanagh (13)
Queen Katharine Academy, Walton

SPLIT PERSONALITY

Entering this super atmosphere, we meet the hero of this city, RX, who was running away from people. It was found out that RX was a villain but also a hero. RX had a split personality, half hero, half villain, but he was a villain in his second form. RX had two forms: half was evil, and half was good. To take away the evil half, he would have to kill himself, but he wanted to live. However, people wanted to execute him, so the evil was gone.

You are reading this on the day of my execution.

(*Lights close*)

Raheel Kazim (14)
Queen Katharine Academy, Walton

THE DRAGON

A young man in his late thirties comes back from work and is shocked to see large footprints outside his house. Suddenly just before he's about to set foot in his house it explodes and sets on fire. He gets launched into the air and gets bashed against a tree. As he struggles to get up he sees a large fierce fire-breathing dragon. His eyes widen and he lets out a small gasp and without thinking he jumps up and runs limping but the dragon sets him on fire. He runs around in agony but the dragon has suddenly disappeared.

Laibah Arif (11)

Queen Katharine Academy, Walton

THE APP

Ignoring the warning, I downloaded the app. I felt a sudden breeze hit my shoulders. I looked back at my phone. It said two words that will haunt me forever. 'Turn around!'
As I turned my head ever so slightly, there was a man standing in front with a full black outfit and a gun pointing at me. I couldn't bear to look them in the eye, so I turned back to the app. It now said something totally different. It said, 'Look again'. So I did. The gun was now pointed at my phone. I looked, then I woke up.

Willow Smith (11)
Queen Katharine Academy, Walton

IT WASN'T A JOKE

Ignoring the warnings, I downloaded the app. It was the afternoon and I was hanging out with my friend, Jack. It started off fun, but then we were both bored to death, so we downloaded this app on my phone.

We saw ads for it everywhere and we thought it was fake, but to our knowledge, it wasn't. It was an app that took you to random locations and apparently, there were zombies there. It gave us a location and since we thought it was fake, we went there. Once we got there, to our surprise, there were dead zombies.

Maya Zasada (12)
Queen Katharine Academy, Walton

EXTINCTION OF HUMANS

Every clock had stopped...

At first, nobody had noticed. But after an hour, people were confused as to why the clocks weren't working. On the news, they were talking about why the clocks were not working. It was because the Earth stopped moving. People did not know what to do about it. Everyone was shocked because after two hours the sun exploded and Earth was full of darkness. People were dying quickly. Lots of buildings were falling and breaking other buildings. The moon exploded into two. Humans were extinct.

Eryk Hoscilowicz (11)
Queen Katharine Academy, Walton

THE GLITCH?

Time ticked. I sat, tied up. I knew too much about the world. I knew this would happen. A single raindrop fell across the window, glistening and glimmering like a diamond fragment. We were living in a time loop. I was the only human that knew.

I saw an agent approach me. They held a rifle which was large and contained plenty of bullets. The gun fired and a loud sound echoed. I looked at the floor and saw my lifeless body, blood oozing from it. I was dead. I was a ghost. However, if we lived in a time loop, then...

Minahil Tahir (12)
Queen Katharine Academy, Walton

INTO THE TREE

I didn't move but my reflection did. The clocks had stopped and everyone was frozen except me but why? And how was I the only one moving? Looking around, trying to see if anyone could move, I found something. Something fast and discombobulated. I tried catching up to it but it was no use. The figure got away. The last time I saw it, the figure ran into a tree. I slowly walked to the oak tree and pressed onto it, trying to find the small figure. Suddenly, my hand fell in and I was pulled through the grand oak tree.

Evie Feerick (13)
Queen Katharine Academy, Walton

TRAVELLING THROUGH TIME

Suddenly, I was travelling through time. My head twitched. I saw something in the corner of my eye. I glazed in the fear. An alien appeared out of the corner. My heart stopped, it seemed like hours passed in the space of two minutes. The aliens started approaching me. I started backing away but it seemed to get faster towards me. I tried fighting but it got scared and ran but I trapped it. As soon as I got it, I studied where it came from and what was going on. All of a sudden my house got chucked by something bigger.

Dejvi Alijaj (13)
Queen Katharine Academy, Walton

MAN TO THE SLAUGHTER

I buried it but it was back...

Ever since I killed my husband for cheating, I've had the best life! I got a job as a baker and married a sweet guy!

Anyway, it was a late night. I was packing up my things when I heard a loud *bang!* I ran to the scene and I discovered nothing! I assumed I was tired so I jumped in my car and drove away.

Suddenly, I saw my dead husband's soul coming closer until everything turned black! I opened my eyes slightly and there were police and ambulance sirens...

Liya Tawfeq (11)

Queen Katharine Academy, Walton

THE LOST GIRL

Hi, I'm Kyra, Let me tell you what happened. It all started a month ago. I was going to New York for college but I live in London. I was on the plane. Then it crashed. I woke up. I was on an island. No! I was supposed to be in New York, I started walking and saw my dad. He was a king. "How? What - how are you king?" I was a princess, omg.
So I started exploring. *I love this island. One day, this has to be mine.*
After spending about a couple of years on the island, I became Queen Kyra.

Ummayyah Ali (12)
Queen Katharine Academy, Walton

IT STARTS AT THE END

Ignoring the warnings, I clicked install. Surely it can't be that bad, right? Besides, I was aching with curiosity. I felt a jolt of nervousness as I signed up. As much as I wanted to know when I was going to die, I was still anxious. Then I saw my time; my heart dropped.

Panicked, I ran out of my building, got in my car and drove to the pier. My heart was pounding. I felt dizzy and faint. I sat down, legs dangling over the cliff edge. Loud noises, head spinning. A large, strong gust of wind. I'm gone...

Olivia-Mae Brudenell (12)
Queen Katharine Academy, Walton

THE PICTURES

Ignoring the warnings, I downloaded the app. The next morning the app automatically opened, making me inspect it. The app was named Photobombed. I picked up my phone whilst still suspicious of it. I thought it was a camera but I was wrong. As I went to take a photo a loud *bang* shot my house I selected a killer filter and posed. Then and there, someone with a knife burst into my room. Luckily I was downstairs. As I found a hiding spot, they started walking downstairs. I took another photo. That was a mistake.

Alastair Green (12)
Queen Katharine Academy, Walton

END OF THE END

Five years ago, a nuclear explosion wiped out most of mankind. Those who remained unlocked powers and fought to the death. Five years I spent honing my powers and killing everyone else. Now it was just me and my opponent. This would be easy. My powers allowed me to copy the powers of others, which may have been rubbish but I awakened it and now could be called a god. I took out my knife. My left foot went forward, then my right. In an instant, I was in front of my opponent. I stabbed him. I looked around. I smiled.

Tuaha Saqib (12)
Queen Katharine Academy, Walton

UNTITLED

Am I the only one? As a bit of background, I love to draw! But recently I haven't enjoyed it. It seems that whenever I draw something, it becomes a reality. Like, for example, I drew a dog playing in the park. Then when I went to the park, the dog was there playing. There have been a lot more but there are just too many to say.

One day I was bored and started drawing. I was in my own world. When I realised what I had drawn, I was on a hike and I fell off a cliff!

I'm going on a hike in an hour!

Sofie Hollis (13)
Queen Katharine Academy, Walton

END OF THE WORLD

One day, a cyber attack happened. All the phones were down. There was a knock at the door: a man and a girl. You offer them a place to stay. You wake up to a loud ringing noise that burns your ears when listened to.

The next day, you and your friend go to the woods. Your friend gets bitten by an alien bug. You both go home to the friendly people. A plane has crashed into your house. They lie there, dead. You run to the neighbour's house with your friend and go into their bunker, hopefully leaving soon.

Gracie-May McGill (12)
Queen Katharine Academy, Walton

THE SISTERS THAT WERE GOOD SKATERS

The night just started at 6pm and Bella and Megan were doing their skates up. The music was blasting out and the lights were brighter than the sun. They knew it was gonna be a good night. Megan went to the rink and Bella followed her. They went backwards and sideways and spun around in circles. Then their fave song came on and they went into the middle of the rink and danced their hearts out like they did every Friday at 6pm.

"It was so fun!" Bella said to Megan. She said the same back to Bella.

Bella Nicholls (13)
Queen Katharine Academy, Walton

WHAT IF YOU KNEW THE WORLD WOULD END?

It was a cold, dark, stormy evening. Tonight will be the last normal night for a long time. Later that night, I prepared for what was about to happen at some point tomorrow.
I woke up in the morning and packed, putting things ready to leave home and not come back for a very long time.
Then all of a sudden, a lot of meteors fell out of the sky and nearly killed me, and then a tsunami happened. It was as tall as Big Ben. I couldn't believe it was really happening.
It was the end of the world.

Spencer Currie (13)
Queen Katharine Academy, Walton

THE JAMAICAN WAY

Once upon a time, in the mountains, a young Jamaican boy was playing with his blue football. By the way, he was ten years old, so he was with his mum. Later on, the mum went. Then, after five minutes, his ball fell down the mountain all the way to the bottom. While he was coming down, he spotted a football with a Jamaican hat, so in the end, he said, "That's the Jamaican way!"
He went back up the mountain, and then his mum came. He ate some cookies and started playing football with her.

Ricardo Christie-Mpitu (13)
Queen Katharine Academy, Walton

IS THIS REAL?

Everything had stopped apart from me. *Is this real? Am I dreaming? I have to be. Am I doing this?* I could do anything I wanted. Then everything resumed. I could stop evil with this. But I'm just a person and nobody. It was worth a shot. Two weeks later, people were calling me a superhero, a beacon of light. A man on the news was shooting lasers. I had to get there. When I got there, I stopped time and barraged him in the face with my fists. He shot his laser. It hit me in the chest. What?

Tommy-Lee Gates (12)
Queen Katharine Academy, Walton

END OF HUMANITY!

Once upon a time, in the year 8450, humanity was on the brink of extinction. The nuclear war was going on for months. The residents of the world were in hiding. The nuclear superpowers were at war with each other. Most of the world was dead. The remainder of people had to scavenge for food and water. We had to hide out in fallout shelters. All of us had no way to contact anyone. If this war went on for any longer then the world would fall to darkness and death. This world was doomed. We all were gonna die!

Liam Wright (13)
Queen Katharine Academy, Walton

THE BOMB

About 300 years ago a bomb hit the world, leaving two people alive. Now the planet is left looking worse than a rubbish dump left for years! The government has now decided that all the people on Mars will go to the new and improved Planet Earth to start a new life. This is because a robot was found and it was trying to fly to Mars and kill the whole human existence. If the robot reaches Mars before everyone escapes, all of the planets will explode. All people start to pack up for the long journey to Earth.

Evie McKimmie (12)
Queen Katharine Academy, Walton

THE BOY THAT WAS ALL PART OF A DREAM

A schoolboy was murdered and two weeks later a new kid came to his school. Little did they know, they would make a shocking discovery. He looked similar to him but he was never told that. A couple of months later, he was never seen again, and it turns out he was never there. He was just in their heads. It was the ghost of Bill the schoolboy and he never existed. The parents of the boy died with no reason to. It turns out they died ages ago and were rewatching their life story before going to Heaven.

Kayla Kelly (12)
Queen Katharine Academy, Walton

SHE IS BACK

We buried it, but it was back by the door the next day. My cat, dead, aged only two, my poor baby! I arrived home after school at 3:54 to find my cat's body unresponsive in her favourite spot, frozen. A million thoughts rushed through my head at that moment. We buried her by her own family tree on the same day. I went to sleep after tears ran down my face. I woke up from a nightmare in the middle of the night, sweating and drowning for a weight on me. It was my cat, my baby. But was it really?

Renata Ciumac (14)
Queen Katharine Academy, Walton

TIME TRAVELLING

One dark, gloomy night, I'm coming home from work and decide to take the shortcut through the alleyway. I hear a zapping sound coming from a garbage bin. I open it and see a raccoon has teleported through. I go inside and press a button. It looks like I'm in space.

Finally, I'm here. I open the door and bullets pass my head. I jump into a ditch. I'm in the trenches. I must be in WWII. A Nazi soldier aims a gun at my face and shouts in German. He shoots me. My eyes black out.

Aden Makauskas (13)

Queen Katharine Academy, Walton

THE PARKOUR MAN

Hi, my name is Dainton. One day, I was looking on YouTube and was intrigued by parkour, so I tried it in my room every day until I got it. I went and climbed a building and jumped to each building. I got this weird feeling that if I fell, I wouldn't get hurt, and then my body went purple, so I tried jumping off the building and I couldn't feel pain when I hit the ground. My eyes went black the moment I realised I had superpowers, and I thought I could do more magical stuff than that!

Dainton Tee (14)
Queen Katharine Academy, Walton

THE MAGIC PUPPY

One day, a little puppy was wandering around a field all alone until an old man found it. The dog had a limp and it looked like it had been outside for a long time. So the old man decided to take the dog home. He waddled back to his little bungalow. He put the dog in the bath and gave it some food, water and a toy to play with. Suddenly, its feet started to lift up from the ground and started to speak. The old man grabbed his phone and started to record it and post it online. He turned famous.

Evie Bass (12)
Queen Katharine Academy, Walton

THE UNFORGETTABLE SCIENCE LAB

Hello, my name is Henry. I had always lived a normal life until, well, the incident. My father at the time was a scientist who would take me to work with him every day. One day, I was playing around with the chemicals and *bam!* They had split all over my face and body. I was woken up by my father's screams but as I stood up, my feet lifted from the ground and I could fly. The burns over me made me seem like a monster, hence they called me Horrid Henry. I flew out of there and hid.

Regina Phiri (13)
Queen Katharine Academy, Walton

TAKE ME AWAY

"It's my birthday, finally!"
I was overjoyed for what I thought would be a great day. I ran down the stairs faster than a cheetah. To my surprise, my parents were gone. "Mum, Dad!" I shouted in fear when I saw a note that read 'Take me away, away you'll take me. Not too long before you're gone too'.
In pure distress, I ran out of my front door and there was no one there. I looked to the sky and what I saw next I can't even explain.

Taylor Baines (13)
Queen Katharine Academy, Walton

THE STRANGE DREAM

One night, before I went to sleep, I talked to my friends. I fell asleep. The next morning seemed perfect. I looked so good. My favourite dish was prepared in the kitchen and I even got a message from my crush asking me out. I went to school.

There, everything was strange, and by that, I mean that everyone was the opposite gender. I could barely recognise them. As I entered the school, I was now a boy and my crush was a girl...

But then I woke up, and I was late for school.

Denisa Dorobantu (13)
Queen Katharine Academy, Walton

THE REVENGE OF MY LITTLE SISTER

It is time for the revenge of my little sister's death. I went to a place which was like a castle. I opened the giant door and saw so many skeletons all over the place. When I went upstairs, I saw them, witches. But as one of them turned, I hid, but it was too late. All of them started chasing me with their powers but I stood up and started using my magic. When I started flying, my eyes lit up and I burned all the place as I heard them all scream and their flesh burned.

Cadi Balde (13)
Queen Katharine Academy, Walton

THE MAGICAL BOOK

Hi, my name is Aayan. I am fourteen years old. Two or three weeks ago, I was going to school and there was a stranger who was trying to sell a book but no one was buying that book. I went to him and asked about the book. He said it was a magical book and I thought it was interesting, so I bought it. I drew a note of five pounds. It was in front of me. I started drawing lots of things like cars, money, etc. Suddenly, my alarm went off. I woke up and saw it was a dream.

Aayan Shahid (14)
Queen Katharine Academy, Walton

WEIRD DREAM

Today was the first day of high school and only one of my friends came with me. I was on my way to my lesson when I saw this girl. It had looked as if she was on fire and true fact, she was. I don't know why but I just walked past as if it was nothing. My friend and I were in the same lesson and we noticed something weird. Our teacher kept glitching, so I couldn't tell if she was real or not. My friend then looked at me with a grin and shot me. It was a dream.

Kaylub Thurston (13)
Queen Katharine Academy, Walton

DEATH'S MARK

The mark's gone. It vanished after taking her life. I'm standing by the grave she's buried under, tears falling silently. I remember the day it all started. The black skull on my hand, my fate decided. I kept it secret, or I thought I did. Somehow, she knew. She knew I was chosen. I should have believed her. She always said she would take her own life to save me. Of course, I thought she was only joking. Well, I guess I was wrong...

Cerys Jenner (13)
Queen Katharine Academy, Walton

A GLITCH IN THE SYSTEM

"You're early," said Death. "What happened?"
"I was walking and then I appeared here," I said.
"Hmm, I wonder what happened. I know, it was a glitch in the system," Death exaggerated.
"So what happens? Do I go back to the living or not?" I said.
"You get to choose to go back or not," he said.
"Okay, then I choose..."

Wiktor Wilk (13)
Queen Katharine Academy, Walton

THE MILK RUN

"Well... I suppose it started this morning," I told Death.
I got out of bed on my favourite day of the week, Saturday.
Mum had asked me to go on a milk run, so I did.
I stepped outside and admired the world on my voyage.
That was until I reached Camden Town.
It was pandemonium. Flying cars everywhere, roads
completely modified, glass buildings towered, with a
sonorous uproar.
Yet, nobody was talking; all noises were coming from
devices. People stood only centimetres apart, texting.
I got distracted and foolishly tripped onto the road...
There I was, Death before me now.
"I tripped. That's what happened."

Ejaz Khan (14)
Regent High School, Camden

THE FATEFUL OWN GOAL

The game tied, 4-4. Time slipped through Muhsin's fingers. Muhsin resurfaced memories of his younger self; in a room where drawings adorned the walls and predicted the future. In it, he saw drawings of cryptic and prophetic feats, until he saw himself, a villain scoring an own goal. Blood pounded in his head, haunting him. Shuddering, Muhsin focused on avoiding it.

Suddenly, the ball hurled towards him and met his foot...
own goal!

His teammates looked furious as if they wanted to rip him apart, bone by bone.

Muhsin felt a sudden excruciating pain and dropped dead, exactly like the drawings. Fate had struck!

Abdul Yahya (13)
Regent High School, Camden

UNTITLED

The bright sunlight didn't arrive that cold morning, neither did the bluebird's song, greeting the rise of day.

Even in silence, you'd expect some sort of disturbance in the air, yet the world was soundly asleep. All the clocks had stopped working, humanity was unconsciously chasing illusions, losing so much time, true joy and fulfilment in the process.

One must inhale deeply, realise one's luck in breathing in glorious air, full of life.

One may not have enough time to *save the world*, yet nevertheless one must make sure to experience as much as possible in the limited time of life.

Angelica Kazankova (14)
Regent High School, Camden

SHATTERED SHADOW

I didn't move, but my reflection did, tentatively gripping my arm with its icy fingers. It then yelped a blaring groan and loped soundlessly into the perpetual darkness.

Despair awaited me, my other side was sightless and impenetrable. Evil was lurking in every corner and it was bound to get me next.

"Don't get close to me!" I screamed as my echo amplified into the musky sky like the haunted moan of death.

On the far shore. It was there, its mouth dripping, staring into the sun with its eyes dead white.

"Maybe next time," it mumbled and silently lurched away.

Shezmin Begum (13)
Regent High School, Camden

THE MERGE

Suddenly, I was travelling through time, watching my whole world fall apart. Reminiscing about the minutes before disaster, I realised what had happened; they didn't manage to stop the machine on time. I slowly drifted away, landing with a painful thump in a futuristic-looking city. I walked around with different types of people catching my eye. This place was peculiar and these people knew it. While walking, I could hear other people talking about something familiar, 'The Merge'. I learnt the machine was made to merge realms. It dawned on me, I was completely alone and needed to survive.

Sara Ahmed (13)
Regent High School, Camden

THE NEVER-ENDING MIRROR MAZE

I didn't move but my reflection did. My heart sank. Doubting what I had seen, I froze in silence. Contemplating whether it was just another child innocently trying to escape the mirror maze.

There. Again.

An enigmatic figure rapidly scurried by. Echoing around the walls, my name was perpetually whispered. Wanting to scream yet no sound came. Heavily panting and desperately trying to escape, all I wanted was to leave this horror house. My eyes drenched in tears, body filled with nausea. My head began to feel heavy. My legs eventually collapsed. I had lost all hope of ever escaping.

Maya Ullah (14)
Regent High School, Camden

MR GRIM

Grim knew he had this appointment with Death. He hated everything. His heart was darker than obsidian and his soul was polluted with shadows.

One day, in his basement, he discovered a portal glimmering in the corner. His sinister curiosity moved him. As he edged closer, it started reeling him in until the force was too strong. He was summoned into a new dimension full of demons and hellfire; there to pay for his sins. As he crawled, he watched the eternal blaze beneath him. He fell, Death taking him under his everlasting and dark, infinite cloak.

Kassim Kassim (14)
Regent High School, Camden

REVENGE

My whole life flashed before me and then I woke up. A nostalgic feeling came over me as I realised I was in my bed from my room when I was fifteen. All my memories flooded my brain.

Then a screen popped up in front of me, saying to return to the future I must kill the person who ruined my life. I was infuriated as I remembered him.

I searched everywhere, hiding a sharp dagger, ready to slaughter him.

Then he was in front of me. Reflexively I stabbed him, but I didn't return.

The screen came back, saying there was a glitch.

Immanuel Chella (13)
Regent High School, Camden

A DARK REFLECTION

My mind flooded with different emotions. My reflection? I was not crying. Bangs of bombs! It was another girl, a few years older than me. Could it be me? December came; the sun was beaming, but people weren't. My heart was pounding, pounding like a firework that was going to explode. A moment later, I felt like an outcast. What was I supposed to do in this obliterated world? I needed help, and if this old, vintage mirror was warning me, I should listen. This was a huge warning, one that would change the world only in a few years to come.

Sannah Yaqub (14)
Regent High School, Camden

UNTITLED

I had three years left, according to the app. Clearly, I was lied to. It arrived many years before the due date. It was an ordinary Monday. The streets of London were as loud as a packed football stadium. I was walking, when suddenly my heart started to burn. My vision started to disappear at the speed of light. Death introduced itself to me, earlier than expected. It came, ruthlessly ripping my soul out. As much as I tried to resist, there was no use. It held onto me, making sure it wouldn't lose me. It had trapped me forever.

Sami Rahman (14)
Regent High School, Camden

MIRROR, MIRROR... A SOUL PIECED TOGETHER

I felt incomplete, as if a piece of me was missing. I stared in horror at the translucent figure glaring back at me. Why had Death chosen me? Surely, there had been a mistake. I attempted to communicate with my reflection through some ritual, but ended up with wailing so deafening the mirror could have shattered to pieces. Without any warning, my soul seeped out of me, evaporating into the mirror, leaving a lifeless body behind. This was a reality fate had chosen. Death is inevitable, but this - this was me becoming whole again...

Zaira Harris (13)
Regent High School, Camden

TRUTH TELLER

It had been a long day, my head throbbed in agony.

I went to the art gallery to clear my mind. I saw someone painting, so I went to look.

I saw something. I saw myself. It was me in the art gallery. I was terrified, but then I realised the drawings predicted the future.

Besides what I saw, I dropped my phone, and my mouth opened. I was frozen in fear, lost for words.

Hurriedly, I sprinted but it was too late. The sun erupted in flame, but not before an unheavenly bang was heard. All hope was lost.

Karim Isli (13)
Regent High School, Camden

YOUNG WRITERS INFORMATION

We hope you have enjoyed reading this book – and that you will continue to in the coming years.

If you're the parent or family member of an enthusiastic poet or story writer, do visit our website **www.youngwriters.co.uk/subscribe** and sign up to receive news, competitions, writing challenges and tips, activities and much, much more! There's lots to keep budding writers motivated!

If you would like to order further copies of this book, or any of our other titles, then please give us a call or order via your online account.

Young Writers
Remus House
Coltsfoot Drive
Peterborough
PE2 9BF
(01733) 890066
info@youngwriters.co.uk

Join in the conversation!
Tips, news, giveaways and much more!

f YoungWritersUK   **𝕏** YoungWritersCW

⊚ youngwriterscw   **♪** youngwriterscw

SCAN TO
WATCH THE
GLITCH VIDEO!